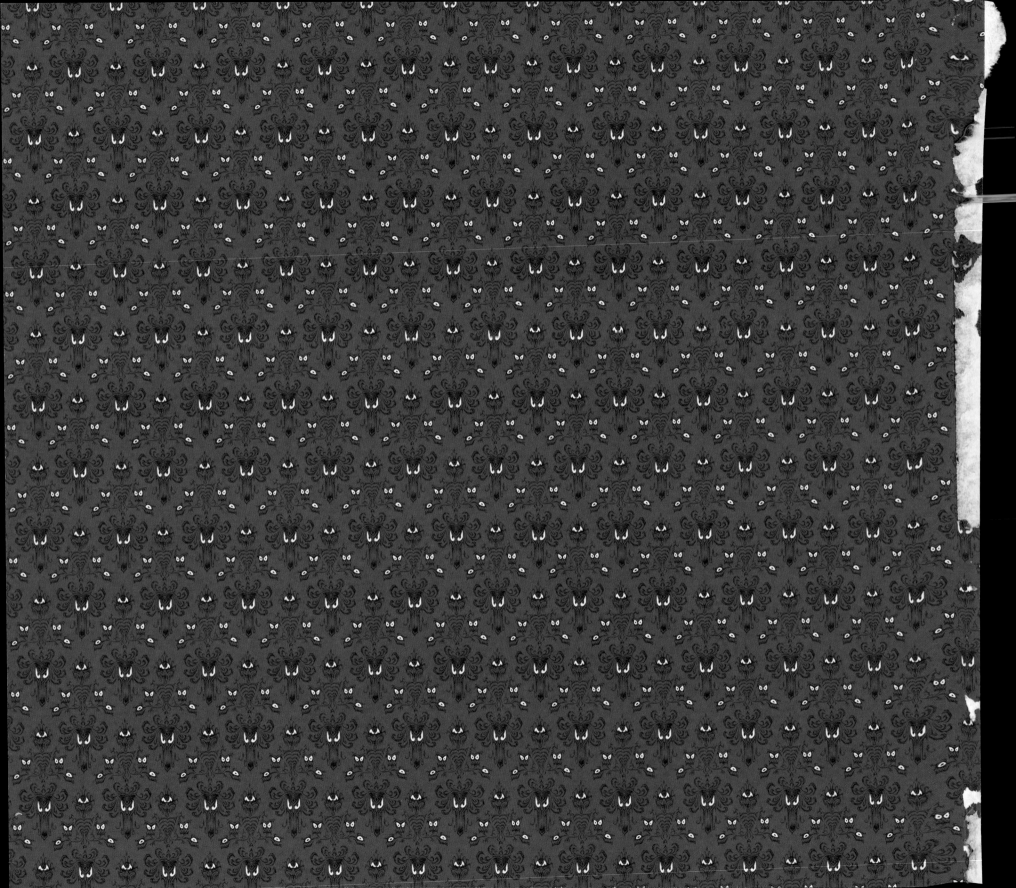

Editorial by Eric Geron
Design by Lindsay Broderick

"Grim Grinning Ghosts"
Music by Buddy Baker
Lyrics by Xavier Atencio
Published by Walt Disney Music
Company (ASCAP).
© Renewed. All Rights Reserved.
Lyrics reprinted by permission.

Executive Producer Randy Thornton
Mixed by Randy Thornton and Jeff Sheridan
Mastered by Jeff Sheridan

Printed in the United States of America
First Hardcover Edition, July 2016
1 3 5 7 9 10 8 6 4 2
FAC-03427-16141
ISBN 978-1-4847-2785-0

DISNEP PARKS

PRESENTS

The Haunted Mansion

REST
IN
PEACE

DEAR BELOVED
GEORGE

QUICK
SAND

Music by Buddy Baker

Lyrics by Xavier Atencio

Illustrations by James Gilleard

DISNEP PRESS

Los Angeles • New York

Happy haunts materialize . . .

Grim Grinning Ghosts come out to socialize!

Now don't close your eyes and don't try to hide,
or a silly spook may sit by your side—
shrouded in a daft disguise,
they pretend to terrorize. . . .

As the moon climbs high o'er the dead oak tree,

Spooks arrive for the Midnight spree.

When you hear the KNeLL of a RequieM beLL, weird gLows gLeaM where spirits dweLL.

RestLess bones etheReaLize,
Rise as spooks of every size. . . .

MoRTaLs pay a token fee....

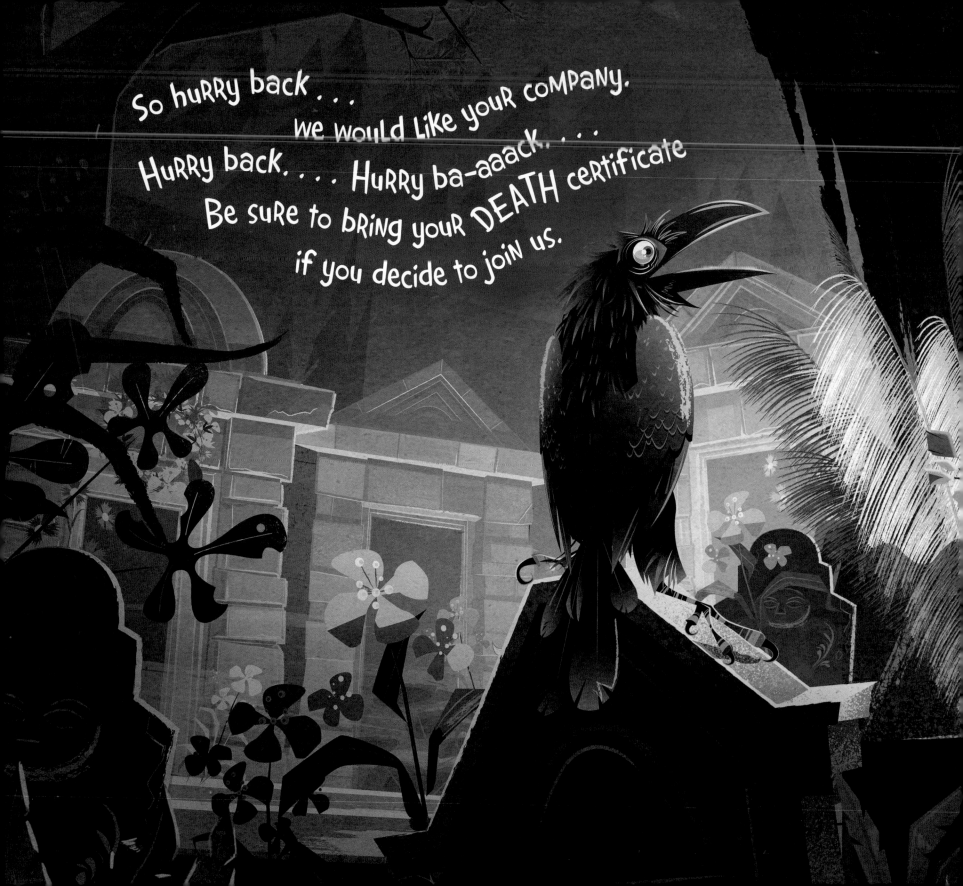

Make final arrangements now.
We've been DYING to have you.

THE END?

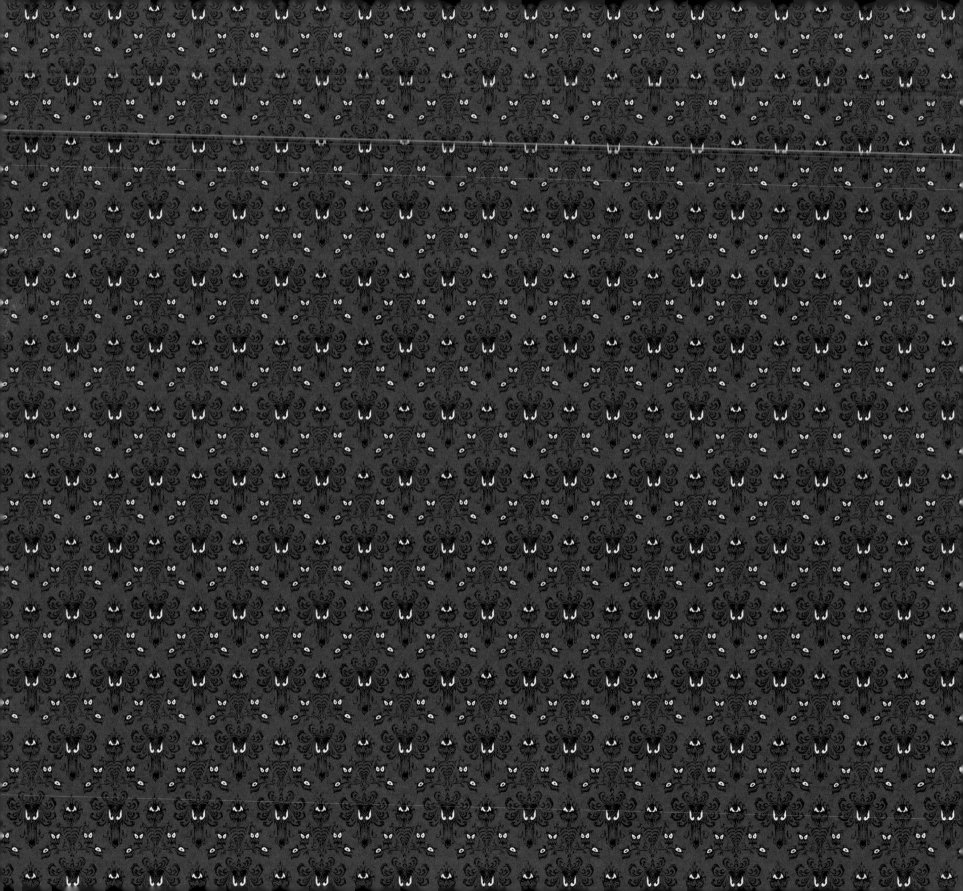